PERSEPHONE

Written by Sally Pomme Clayton

Illustrated by Virginia Lee

Eerdmans Books for Young Readers

Grand Rapids, Michigan ❖ Cambridge, U.K.

Persephone was playing in the fields,
running, laughing, and chasing her friends. The sun
felt warm on her bare arms, and the long grass tickled her
legs. It was spring. Brightly colored flowers grew all around
her. She gathered them into the folds of her gown.
Brilliant crocuses, violets like gems, narcissi nodding their heads,
green shoots of barley pushing out of the ground — Persephone
picked and picked and picked, leaving her friends far behind.

Suddenly there was a rumbling sound. The earth trembled and the ground opened up. A golden chariot pulled by four black horses appeared from beneath the earth. Hades, the King of the Underworld, shook the reins.

"Whoa, my beasts! Who is this beauty? A living girl to be my bride?"

He reached out, plucked Persephone from the ground, and pulled her into his chariot.
"You will be Queen and light up my kingdom," he said.
Persephone began to cry. But Hades cracked his whip and the horses galloped off.

They rode and rode, until they came to a pool. A sparkling spring of water bubbled up from underground. It was a gateway to the Underworld. Hades pulled his horses to a stop.

A water nymph with flowing hair and dripping dress rose up from the pool.

"This is my home," she said. "No one enters here by force." And she stretched out her watery arms to block their path.

"You cannot make this girl go with you," she said.

But Hades threw his golden whip into the water. It struck the bottom of the pool, and a door appeared. Then Hades and Persephone plunged down to the Underworld.

They raced along beneath towering rocks. They passed snakes and
crawling creatures. They rode past boiling lakes and fields of lava.
"Now that you are Queen, all this belongs to you," said Hades.

"Look!" He pointed to the earth gleaming with gold,
to lumps of crystal winking beside the road.
    But Persephone did not care. A shadow fell across her face,
and stayed there.

Meanwhile, out in the sunshine,
Persephone's friends stopped playing and looked around
for their missing friend. When they saw a heap of flowers lying on the
ground, their laughter died away. They ran to Persephone's mother and
exclaimed, "She's gone — Persephone's gone!"

Mother Demeter, Goddess of Earth,
called and called for her daughter, but there was no reply.
So she took a burning torch in each hand and set off to search for
Persephone. Demeter walked through long hot days and frosty nights looking
for her. She walked and walked for weeks and months. She walked around
the whole Earth, but she did not find her daughter.

Exhausted, Demeter came to a pool and sat down to rest. She saw a ribbon floating on the water. She reached across and pulled the ribbon out of the water. Tears sprang from her eyes.

"This is Persephone's ribbon. I tied it in her hair myself," cried the goddess. "Oh, where is my daughter?"

The water bubbled and the nymph rose up.

"Great Goddess, I know where your daughter is. Hades has taken her to his kingdom. I swam down to the bottom of the pool and peeped into the Underworld and I saw her sad face.

"Persephone is Queen, sitting on a throne of gold. But she neither eats nor sleeps. She only weeps."

"Curse you, cruel Earth!" she cried. "You don't deserve to bear fruit if you keep my daughter underground."

Demeter pulled her cloak around her shoulders, and a cold wind began to blow. It tore leaves from the trees and plants from their roots. The earth became frozen, hard as stone. Flowers, fruits, and barley lay hidden underground.

A year passed and nothing on Earth grew. It was a year of
hunger and misery. It was winter all the time. No one recognized
the Great Goddess, wrapped in her cloak, weeping and waiting for
the world to die of hunger.

Father Zeus, God of the Sky, looked down and saw that the Earth was dying. He called for his swiftest messenger.

"Hermes, you travel the world. You know the way to every secret place. Find Persephone and bring her back. Then Demeter, Goddess of Growth, will make Earth green again."

Hermes put on his winged sandals and magic helmet. He took up his golden wand coiled round with snakes, and in a flash rose up into the air.

He flew, swift as the wind, between sky and sea and over rock. Like lightning, he traveled through clouds. In an instant he was underground, in Hades' dark kingdom.

"I come with a message," said Hermes. "Father Zeus calls Persephone home. Earth is dying. Nothing grows without Demeter's help. Hades, you must let her go."

Hades was silent. Persephone held her breath, waiting for him to speak, and the Underworld waited, too. At last Hades said, "Persephone, flower of my life, you have made my gloomy kingdom bright. Everything shines while you are here. But because I love you, I will let you go. Let no one say that Hades is a cruel king. Go home, Persephone, be sad no longer."

Persephone leapt to her feet.

"Wait, my Queen," said Hades. He lifted a golden plate piled with juicy seeds. "All this time no food has passed your lips. Please, eat before you go."

The seeds were red and seemed to glow. Persephone suddenly felt hungry. She reached out, took three seeds, and popped them into her mouth. She crushed the seeds against her tongue and a sweet, tangy juice burst inside her mouth. Persephone licked her lips.

Then Hermes took her hand and in an instant, swift as wind, they flew from dark to light.

At that moment, Demeter looked up and there
stood Persephone!

She flung her arms around her daughter and hugged
her tight. Then, Demeter took the tattered ribbon and
tied it in Persephone's hair. Mother and daughter
clasped hands and walked home.

With each step Persephone took, the grass grew,
buds opened, flowers bloomed, and green shoots
of barley pushed out of the earth. The air was
filled with the sound of birds singing.
Persephone had returned, and
spring had come at last.

At home, Demeter spread the table with fresh bread,
white cheese, dark olives, and cool glasses of barley water.
  "It's so lovely to be home," laughed Persephone.
"I'm starving!" And she reached towards the food.
  "You didn't eat, my daughter, did you?" asked Demeter.
"You didn't eat the food of the Underworld?"

"No, Mother. No food passed my lips," said
Persephone, sucking on an olive. "Oh! Except. . ."

"Except what?" said Demeter.

"Three pomegranate seeds. Three tiny little seeds."
Then Demeter began to cry.

"Oh, Persephone! The food of the dead must not
be eaten by the living. For those three seeds, my
daughter, I will lose you."

And so for three months of each year Persephone
must return to the Underworld. Hades welcomes back
his queen, but when Persephone goes underground,
winter comes to the Earth.

When the three months are over, Persephone returns to
Earth. Ice melts and the ground grows soft. Earth bears
fruit. Demeter hugs her daughter, and picks barley to
make bread. Spring has come again.

A Journey from Death to Life
about the story

In Ancient Greece, the goddesses Demeter and Persephone were honored every year with festivals linked to the cycle of planting, growing, and harvesting. One of the biggest festivals was held in autumn, when women sowed seeds and asked Demeter to make the seeds grow and the harvest fruitful. The mysteries of Demeter also described the journey of growing up — in particular the journey a girl makes to become a woman and a mother. People took part in the festivals hoping to understand the secrets of the myth and to become renewed. One of the most important moments of the celebration was when a priestess held up, for all to see, a stalk of barley: the mystery of life.

The Persephone myth is no longer part of religious

life in Greece, yet it is still part of everyday life. Pomegranate trees grow everywhere there, and the fruit is still connected to both life and death. On New Year's Eve, Greek people crack pomegranates on their doorsteps to bring good luck and success for the coming year. At weddings, pomegranates are broken open and the seeds rolled across the ground to bring a happy marriage and lots of children. At funerals, a special dish called *kollyva* is prepared in honor of the dead. It is made from boiled wheat, sugar, and raisins, and decorated with pomegranate seeds. Even gravestones are decorated with pomegranate fruits and flowers.

The myth of Persephone links life and death in an endless circle.

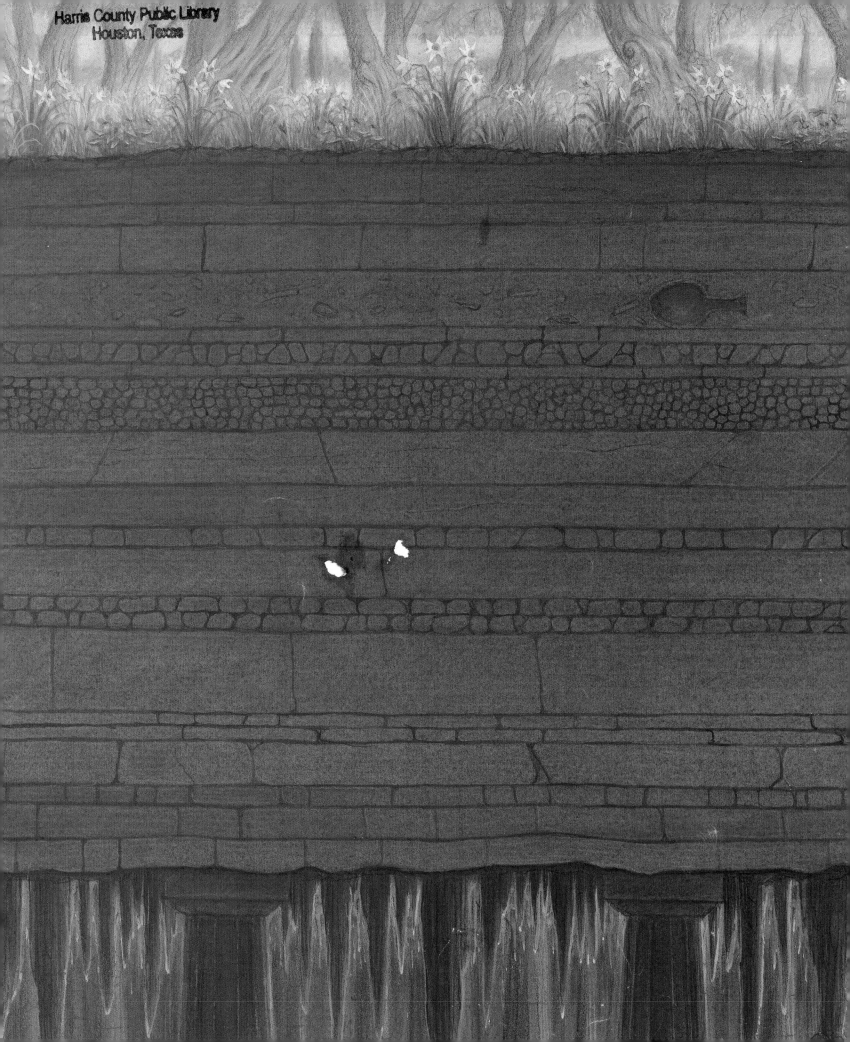